Miss Bindergarten Stays Home from Kindergarten

by **JOSEPH SLATE**

illustrated by **ASHLEY WOLFF**

Dutton Children's Books · New York

For Donna Brooks, who never—well, hardly ever—stayed home from kindergarten

J.S.

For Maria and Pumpkin, the real Miss Bindergartens

A.W.

Text copyright © 2000 by Joseph Slate
Illustrations copyright © 2000 by Ashley Wolff

CIP Data is available.

Published in the United States by Dutton Children's Books,
a division of Penguin Putnam Books for Young Readers
345 Hudson Street, New York, New York 10014
www.penguinputnam.com
First Edition   Printed in U.S.A.
2 4 6 8 10 9 7 5 3 1
ISBN 0-525-46396-8

On Sunday morning, sad but true,
Miss Bindergarten got the flu.
"I'm aching and shaking right down to the bone.
Tomorrow I fear I shall have to stay home."

On Monday—

Miss Bindergarten stays home

from kindergarten.

But at school—

Adam hangs his jacket.

Brenda stores her doll.

Christopher asks,
"Where is Miss B?
I don't see her at all."

"**G**ood morning, kindergarten. I'm sorry to have to say,
Miss Bindergarten called in sick and won't be here today."

"I will be her substitute. My name is Mr. Tusky.
I hope you'll help me through the day—I'm just
a wee bit rusty."

Danny says, "I'll take you round!"

Emily shows off Lizzie.

After lunch, **F**ranny moans, "My tummy hurts. I'm dizzy."

On Tuesday—

Miss Bindergarten *and* Franny

stay home from kindergarten.

But at school—

Gwen fills in the calendar.

Henry names who's who.

Ian cries, "Without Miss B, I don't know what I'll do!"

"I know you may be feeling sad,
but there's not a thing to fear.
Miss Bindergarten sent lesson plans.
I have them all right here."

"We'll sing a song, we'll read a book—
oh, here's what we will do.
Franny and Miss Bindergarten
would love a card from you."

Jessie paints a get-well card.

Kiki prints a letter.

Lenny's card says, "I feel hot, but I hope you're feeling better."

On Wednesday—

Miss Bindergarten, Franny, *and* Lenny

stay home from kindergarten.

But at school—

Matty snacks on crackers.

Noah slurps a sip.

Ophelia shares her celery, carrot sticks, and dip.

Patricia says,
"It's sharing time."

Quentin does a trick.

Raffie's yo-yo twirls and whirls. "Uh-oh," he says. "I'm sick."

On Thursday—

Miss Bindergarten, Franny, Lenny, *and* Raffie

stay home from kindergarten.

But at school—

Mr. Tusky strums and sings.

Sara drums along. **T**ommy claps and **U**rsula taps to Mr. Tusky's song.

That afternoon—

"It's time to go," says Mr. T. "I hate to say good-bye.
    But tomorrow, I'm advised, you'll have a big surprise."

Vicky pulls her parka on.
She's the first in line.

"Mr. Tusky," Wanda says,
"we've had a real nice time."

On Friday—surprise!

Franny, Lenny, Raffie, *and* Miss Bindergarten

are back in kindergarten!

Xavier says, "We missed you!"

Yolanda shouts, "Hooray!"

"Mr. T was fun," says **Z**ach, "but I'm glad you're back today!"

"Thank you, kindergarten. I'm feeling so much better.
I know we're all excited to be once again together.
I never will forget your lovely cards and wishes."

"They made me feel that you were near,
blowing get-well kisses.
And I'm oh-so-very proud, as proud as I can be,
that you worked like little troupers for our dear sub, Mr. T."

stays home from kindergarten . . .

. . . especially Mr. Tusky.